THE PENGUIN DANCE

Eve and Brooke West
Illustrated by David Pollack

HX Book Printing, Guangzhou, China

July 2010   Batch No. 3

ISBN 978-0-615-31749-6

To Daisy

May all your dreams come true.

To Grandma

With love.

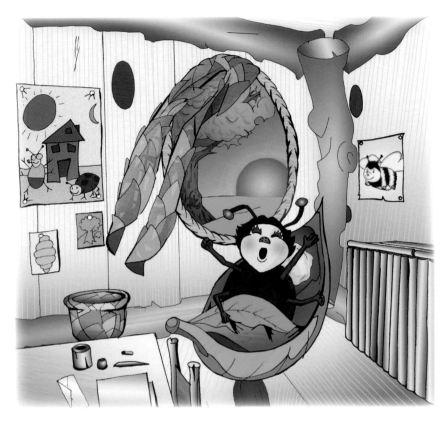

Far away, in Engardia, a magical land that could only be entered in dreams, it was a beautiful Saturday morning. The dew had just set on the grass, the sun was beginning to rise, and Lilly Ladybug awoke from a good night's sleep. Lilly opened her eyes, stretched out her arms, and let out a long yawn.

"It's Saturday morning," she giggled to herself, knowing that Saturday was a play day.

Lilly's bed was made out of a long green leaf, and her head rested on a cotton pillow that the cotton worm had made for her. Her bedroom was the most magical room you could ever imagine: everything was made from leaves and bamboo. Her curtains were woven from brown and green leaves that changed color as the sun glistened on them. The floor was made of pine wood and her desk, with the weekend's homework upon it, was in the corner of the room. Above the desk were drawings that she had drawn in her art class. She could see a view of the beautiful village from her bedroom window, and since her window was an oval shape, without glass, she could always just fly in and out as she pleased.

1

She slid out of bed, and as her feet hit the floor, her pet ants brought her warm slippers to her and slipped them onto her feet. As she skipped toward her bathroom she passed a family photograph of her mother, father, and grandma, and she knew how lucky she was to have a loving family.

The portrait smiled and winked at her as she passed by it, and this made her happy. She also realized how big she was growing! Since female ladybugs are always bigger than males, she was already almost as big as her father. She giggled to herself again.

As she looked in the bathroom mirror, she thought about how she liked being 7. In fact, she liked everything about her life. She smiled from ear to ear, a smile that could lighten up anyone's day. She began to clean her long antennas as the ants ran up the side of the sink to hand her toothbrush to her. She brushed her teeth as she hummed the "Lilly Lullaby" song. When she was done, she looked in the mirror again. The mirror sparkled at her reflection, and gold dust flew all over the bathroom floor.

Lilly then glided to the stairs. Indeed, her stairs were not normal stairs. Yes, there were steps to walk down, but with one quick pull of a wooden lever, the stairs would turn into a slide! Not only was this for fun, but it was also a way to teach ladybugs how to fly. It is hard work when ladybugs fly, because they flap their wings 84 times a second. Lilly slid down the stairway and swooped into her kitchen.

The kitchen table was carved from a beautiful piece of wood, and the chairs around it were shiny leaves that Lilly's family had collected when it was fall. They usually lasted until summer. Her tummy rumbled with hunger for her favorite meal – a meal that most ladybugs loved: aphids. She munched on her aphids, and became more and more excited about her Saturday. She normally went out to play, but on this morning Lilly wanted to do something different. She wanted an adventure, but wasn't quite sure what to do! But she knew just the friend to ask to go with her – her good friend Billy the Bumblebee!

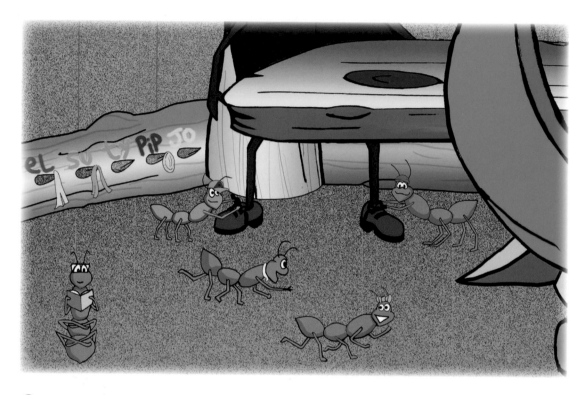

She took her slippers off and slid on her shoes, and the ants ran along and tied up her laces. In the meantime, she wrote a note for her mother and father, telling them she would be back in time for lunch at 12 noon. It was very important that she be home on time, so as not to worry her parents. Lilly snuck out of the house and closed the door gently, being careful not to wake up her sleeping parents.

Billy the Bumblebee lived in a honeycomb, in a beautiful oak tree. The oak tree stood about 60 feet tall, and had honeycombs attached to different branches, with different families of bees living in each honeycomb. Lilly stood in front of the very old tree, and pressed the small button on the tree trunk, which was in fact a glow worm. When pressed, the glow worm would light up and swizzle around the tree, making a high-pitched noise to indicate to the family that there was a visitor. Granddad Berty Bee stuck his head out of one of the honeycomb's holes. Berty was a very old bee, with a long white beard and circle-shaped gold glasses. "Lilly, is that you?" he inquired, his glasses nearly falling off his nose.

"Yes, it's me," she replied with a smile.

With that, the bottom of the tree opened up, revealing an elevator made from bamboo. Lilly stepped inside the elevator, pressed a button, and headed on up to the third branch.

As she stepped away from the elevator, Lilly walked along a thin branch. It was almost like a tightrope. "Good thing I can fly," she thought to herself.

She stood in front of the door. After a moment, Billy's mother opened it. "Morning, Lilly," the tired bumblebee mother said. "Come in."

Everyone was awake in the bees' honeycomb. Inside the comb, it was amazing, as everything in there was made out of wax: tables, chairs, beds...even the TV. The TV, an expensive luxury, was a wax square with a big hole in it. On a regular basis, actors would come and act out scenes behind the square. It was great entertainment. The actors were normally trained ants, and very amusing to watch – always great fun for a Saturday night. Billy's three young brothers were flying around inside, all play fighting with each other; Grandpa was reading a book while sitting on his wax rocking chair; and Daddy Bee was playing his favorite song, "Let It Bee," on a flower-stem saxophone.

Lilly waited for Billy as he flew down from his room. Billy kissed his mother goodbye, saying he would be home for lunch by noon. "Stay safe, and have fun!" she shouted as Billy and Lilly flew down from the honeycomb to the ground.

Billy, like all bees, had four wings, and could always fly slightly faster than Lilly, but not wanting to show her up, he flew at her pace. The truth was, Billy, like all honeybees, could flap his wings 11,400 times a minute, which accounted for the buzzing sound he made.

"What do you want to do today, Lilly?" Billy asked. "We could go play hopscotch. Or go to the market. Or...how about let's go and see the dogs again?"

Smiling, Lilly ignored him and headed in a different direction. "I have something else planned," she said.

Billy looked confused and asked, "Like what, Lilly?"

Billy was always a little bit scared of anything he didn't know.

Lilly turned and looked at Billy: "Okay, Billy," she said, "remember at school, how Mrs. Pillow said that on the first day of spring, the penguins always dance near the ocean? Well, today is the first day of spring!...And I want to see them. Look, I even have this map out of the newspaper I got from Sam; we just head into the woods. I want to go, Billy!"

Billy looked very frightened and confused. "Lilly, we can't. We aren't allowed. No way; I'm not going. Come on, let's go play hopscotch."

Lilly looked at Billy with a serious look in her eyes. "I am going with or without you!" she shouted. She then turned around and walked in the direction of the woods. Billy stood in the same spot for a few moments, wondering whether he should go or not, and as he watched Lilly walk away by herself, he realized he couldn't let her go alone, so he caught up with Lilly to join her on her adventure.

Billy followed Lilly as she led the way. They flew through the village, passing the market stalls, and flying past the school, which looked so empty on the weekend.

Finally, they came to the end of their village, and stood in front of the tall hedge which surrounded the village. It was guarded by The Black Widow Spiders. Billy looked at Lilly and asked, "How are we going to get over the hedge without any help? We are too small, Lilly, and we can't fly that high yet – we haven't been taught."

Lilly giggled and gave Billy a sweet smile, saying, "If you can't go over it, and you can't go through it, well then I guess you'll have to go..."

"...under it!" Billy butted in with a cheeky grin on his face.

Lilly had noticed a small opening in the hedge. When the Widow guards weren't looking, Billy and Lilly squeezed through the small gap and came out the other side. Lilly stood up first, wiped the dirt from her face, looked up, and let out a great big "Wow!"

Billy stood up, not believing what was in front of them: The most magical yet scary-looking woods! Acres and acres of grass and tropical trees and lush greenery lit up their eyes. They headed forwards, on their adventure.

Lilly lead the way; she knew she had to head North, and Billy followed her lead. They passed tall trees, as well as grass that was so thick and tall they had to fly to get over it. They walked and flew, and walked, and flew… but the further they went, the more lost they began to feel. And the more lost they felt, the darker the woods began to seem, and before they knew it, they became scared. The trees were blocking the sky above, so they couldn't see any light. Suddenly, they had reached a dead end. Lilly hugged her own body and shivered. Billy tried to comfort Lilly, who only said, "I'm so confuzzled. I thought we were going the right way – we followed the map." ("Confuzzled" is a mixture of "confused" and "puzzled.") Lilly felt scared and sad.

As they sat on a large gray rock, they noticed – out of nowhere – that swinging from a tree was a strange-looking brown monkey. He swung down from the tree and said, "Hello," as he bounced in front of them.

Lilly and Billy, with a happy but shocked look on their faces, said, "Hello," back to him.

"Hee hee hee hee," the monkey chuckled as he bounced around them in a circle. Then he grabbed a tree branch and hung on it for a few seconds with a cheeky look in his eyes. The monkey's name was Marco – or Marco the Monkey, as he liked to be called. He was flamboyant, and liked to be in the middle of any and all excitement, but underneath his attention-craving side, he was a kind, loyal friend and family member. He lived with his brother, sister, mother, and father. They all lived in a wooden house that was placed in-between two large trees; they had to swing from branch to branch just to enter the tree house. And inside the tree house, it was simply beautiful, for everything was made of banana skins! You see, monkeys never eat the skins of bananas. The beds, the covers, and the sitting area were all banana skin. Everything except for the kitchen, which was made from wood.

Marco kept swinging on the branch until he jumped down in front of them. "What's up?" he shouted.

Being smart, Billy said, "The sky."

"So..." Marco asked, still bouncing all around them, "what are two village animals doing this far out in the woods...? Do your parents know??"

Lilly calmly said, "We are lost. We were looking for the ocean, and we can't find it."

"The ocean! Hey!" Marco said.

Then suddenly he jumped in the air and swung from tree to tree, right into his tree house. Lilly and Billy thought he was gone for good. But seconds later, he jumped down again and presented Lilly with a compass made out of leaves, bananas, and bark. He handed it to Lilly. But just before she could take it out of his hand, Marco quickly put it behind his back. "Not sooo fast! If I give you this, you just head north until you reach the ocean... but I, Marco the Monkey, want something in exchange..."

Lilly and Billy looked at each other.

Marco went on, "You two can both fly...and I cannot! Yes, I can swing and jump from here to there, but I want to fly. When I was a little boy, I used to see the pelicans fly past my tree house and I used to just sit and wish that I could fly. So...well...um...you two can teach me!"

"But you are a monkey!" Lilly said after thinking it over for a while.

"Well, if you're not going to help..." Marco said, and then he started to walk away.

"No, no, we will help you," Lilly and Billy replied together.

Marco turned around with a happy smile on his face, and a look of excitement in his eyes. "Really, will you?" he inquired.

Lilly then jumped down from the rock she'd been peacefully sitting on. "Yes. But first you need to have spots or stripes...See, Billy and I have designs on our backs."

Billy turned around on the rock to show Marco his back. Lilly then picked a berry from a nearby bush and started to squeeze it, producing a red liquid. She then started to draw red stripes on Marco's back.

Marco, being ticklish, giggled, "Hee hee hee."

"There! Now you look like us," Lilly smiled.

Returning to the rock, she stood on her back legs. Billy followed her. "Okay now," said Billy, "just get in this position. It's the position to be in before flying."

Marco did as told.

"Now on the count of 3," said Billy, as Marco watched intently, "jump and flap your wings...uh, I mean your arms, okay?"

Marco nodded.

"1...2...3!"

All at once, Lilly and Billy started to fly. Marco, meanwhile, jumped in the air and flapped his arms as fast as he could.

"I'm a flying monkey!" he shouted, and then he fell to the floor. Laying on his back, Marco let out a vicious sneeze.

"Maybe you...don't feel well?" Lilly asked. "You sound like you have a cold."

"That's impossible," said Marco, jumping to his feet. "Monkeys don't get colds!"

Marco tried to fly over and over again. He was happy to be the center of attention, and although he could not really fly, he felt pleased with himself for trying.

Finally, Marco handed them the compass.

"Thank you," said Marco. "And remember: you are always welcome at Banana Tree Lane."

With that being said, Marco bounced,giggled and jumped up into the trees.

"What a nice guy," Billy whispered to Lilly.

Lilly attached the compass to the end of her antenna, then she and Billy flew north. They flew through the enchanted woods. The trees moved as they passed by, laughing and singing. And the bushes changed into heart shapes, and as the pair kept flying, they could hear the birds singing and the trees making all kinds of sounds. The further they flew, the more the woods seemed to disappear. Soon they could smell fresh seawater.

"I think we're here," Lilly said with excitement.

Suddenly, after they flew over the last bush, their eyes grew big and wide. For the sight before them was a great blue ocean, and miles and miles of sand.

They were so pleased with themselves, they flew all the way down to the ocean and sat on the pink sand. While sitting there, they saw dolphins jumping in the air and singing to each other. "It's better than I could ever have imagined, Billy," Lilly whispered in his ear.

Then, as they stared at the beautiful ocean, they saw that it changed colors – to purple, green, and pink – as the sun danced upon it. They could see that close to them, a bale of turtles were rising out of the ocean and forming a line...In fact, all they could see were the turtles' shells.

The sun was shining so brightly that they could barely see the tall loud penguin jumping out of the ocean. He shot into the air like a rocket, and then landed on a turtle's shell, which was made of 60 strong bones. Then, a moment later, three other penguins followed the first one, all of them doing the same jump out of the ocean!!

The penguins then looked at each other, lifted their flippers in the air, and let out a high-pitched squeak. And with that, the ocean parted – and nearly 50 penguins came up onto the shore and started to dance. They would wave their flippers, stretch their backs, and jump from ocean to land.

Lilly and Billy sat on the beach, looking on in amazement. It was everything that Lilly could have imagined and more. Her smile shone so bright it made her antennae glow orange. She giggled, then she blushed. Although the penguins could not fly, they certainly knew how to dance!

After some time went by, the dancing penguins disappeared into the ocean. Suddenly, Billy noticed that the sun had moved. "It's getting late!" he said in a panic. He and Lilly stood up and looked at each other. "We need to get home, Lilly!" Billy cried.

Lilly nodded her head in agreement. They both took one last look at the ocean, opened up their wings, and flew back toward the woods.

They flew past the trees and bushes, and past Marco's tree house, waving as they did so. They started to get tired, but knew they had to keep flying to avoid being late for their parents. "Come on, Lilly," Billy encouraged.

They flew without rest. At long last, up ahead of them, they could see the hedge bordering their village. They were so very tired, but they just kept flying and flying. As they reached the hedge, they stood in front of it, worrying for a moment because they were so late – and knew that they were going to be in big trouble.

They hunted for the opening they had left through, and found that The Black Widow Guards had covered the Hedge with spider webs! This made for quite a tangled journey back through their opening and to the other side, but they made it through OK. As the pair finally entered their village, they could hear a loud bark coming from in front of them. "What is all this barking about?" Lilly asked.

"It must be bark mail. They are looking for us," said Billy.

In Engardia, bark mail is when the dogs passed important news to each other through barking; sort of like the police, they keep the village safe. The dogs wore green doggy coats when they were on duty, and they regularly ran around the village, helping animals and making sure that everyone was OK. Instead of having walkie-talkies, the dogs would just bark at each other.

"Mommy must have told our friend Scotty's dad that we were missing," Lilly cried.

Lilly and Billy started to fly home as quickly as they could, hearing the dogs howling underneath them. Clearly, everyone was very worried about them. Suddenly they saw their friend Scotty running toward them, with a worried look on his face. Scotty was a beautiful dog who lived with his father, and wanted to make his dad proud by being just like him. His dad, the chief of the police, was a kind and loyal dog, and was always helping everyone out.

"Everyone's soooooo worried about you!" he barked. "It's now 2 o'clock. Where have you been?"

"We got lost," Billy replied.

Scotty let out a long and complicated bark, and with that, all the dogs knew that Billy and Lilly were safe. With that the barking stopped immediately.

"Hop on my back! I'll take you home," said Scotty. And without a second thought, Lilly and Billy jumped on his back! Scotty ran as fast as he could to Billy's house.

As they approached Billy's house, Billy could see his brothers poking their heads out of the honeycomb and making faces. They then danced all around each other to communicate their joy. Billy sighed and jumped off Scotty's back. Scotty was breathing really fast, taking 30 breaths a minute. "Thanks, Scotty," he said. "I'll see you at school, Lilly – unless I get grounded forever!!"

Billy's mother then flew out of their home and wrapped her wings around him. "You silly boy!" she said. "I was so worried."

Scotty trotted quickly to Lilly's house. Lilly was worried about the fact that she had upset her parents, and knew she had to face the consequences. When they got there, Lilly flew down off Scotty's back, took a deep breath, and said, "Thank you."

She approached the front door timidly, and the trees moved out of the way. The ants crawled out from under the door to open it for her.

"Lilly, where have you been?" her father shouted as she walked into the living room where her mother, father, and grandmother were sitting. They were seated on a wooden log, drinking tea from acorn shells.

"Oh, Grandma," cried Lilly, with tears in her eyes. "I forgot you were coming to see us! I was confuzzled this morning."

She ran up to her grandma and gave her a great big hug.

"Lilly, we were VERY worried," her grandma said, offering Lilly a seat next to her.

"You were not home when you promised to be home for lunch, Lilly," her father said with creased eyebrows.

Lilly looked upset and disappointed for not returning home on time, but she was still secretly happy that she'd seen the penguins. "I'm sorry," she said in a humble voice, "we must have lost track of the time."

She felt even more guilty knowing that she'd gone outside the village.

"You must remember, Lilly," her dad said, putting one wing around her, "that when you give your word to be home at a certain time, you must make sure to keep your promise. Otherwise people will not trust you."

She smiled and gave her dad a hug, and her antennae glowed to show her happiness. The family then entered the kitchen to have lunch.

As Lilly washed her favorite green leaf plate, she looked at the reflection of the sun as it shined upon the plate's surface, and for one brief, warm moment it looked like the ocean...

...And she smiled to herself, planning her next adventure.

THE END